Teddy Ruxpin Lullabies

Music by:
George Wilkins

Lyrics by:
Ken Forsse

Illustrations by:
David High
Rennie Rau
Teresa Mazurek
Russell Hicks

The Teddy Ruxpin Theme

Come dream with me tonight
Let's go to far off places
And search for treasures bright

Come dream with me tonight

Let's build a giant airship
And sail into the sky
Let's watch the ground so far below
Let's watch the birds as they fly by

The butterflies in springtime
Will lead us on our way
Exploding dandelions
Will brighten summer's day

And if our dream's a good one
And if our dream is right
Then imagination can be real
If we will dream tonight

Come dream with me tonight
Let's go to far off places
And search for treasures bright

Come dream with me tonight

Let's meet a lovely princess
And stand before a king
Let's dream a great adventure
And let us live a magic dream

The orange leaves of Autumn
Will crackle in the air

In Winter tiny snowflakes
Will sparkle everywhere

And if our dream's a good one
And if we see it through
Then the wondrous dream
we dream tonight
Some day just might come true

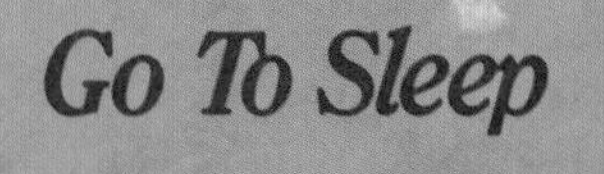

Go To Sleep

We've been tucked in together
The sheets are nice and clean
So close your eyes
Just close your eyes
And we can start to dream

The cows have left the corncrib
A long long time ago
The sheep have left the meadow
They're standing here, you know

They're filling up the bedroom
Those tired little sheep
They wish that you would count them
So they could go to sleep

So close your eyes
It's later than it seems
Close your eyes
It's time for us to dream
We'll drift off together
Like leaves on a stream
So close your eyes
It's time for us to dream

The sandman's also waiting
He's got a job to do
And he can't stand here half
the night
And wait for me and you

It's time to saw some logs now
It's time to get some Z's
It's time for us to crash now
We should be fast asleep

So close your eyes
It's later than it seems
Close your eyes
It's time for us to dream
We'll drift off together
Like leaves on a stream
So close your eyes
It's time for us to dream

We're just two little bedbugs
In need of forty winks
Don't need a drink of water
Brought in from the kitchen sink

We're not up in a treetop
We're safely here in bed
Don't need to make a pit stop
Don't need a story read

So close your eyes
It's later than it seems
...close your eyes
It's time for us to dream
We'll drift off together
Like leaves on a stream
So close your eyes
It's time for us to dream

Sleeping Time

Sleep oh, sleep the night away
The day is far behind us

Sleep oh, sleep the night away
For sleeping time must find us

Treasures that we found today
Will keep until tomorrow

The sandman is just waiting
With dreams that we can borrow

Sleep oh, sleep the night away
The day is far behind us

Sleep oh, sleep the night away
For sleeping time must find us

So cover up your tiny eyes
And dream a nursery rhyme

I'll keep you warm all through the night
For now it's sleeping time

Will You Go To Sleep Before I Do?

I know you're getting tired
You know I'm tired too

So snuggle up and close your eyes
Let's sleep the whole night through

The world is slowing down now
We've had a lovely day
And now we're getting sleepy
Let's dream the night away

Will you go to sleep before I do?
Will you close your eyes real tight?
Will you go to sleep before I do?
And snuggle all through the night?

It's really cozy next to you
On that I can depend
You really take good care of me
I'm glad to be your friend

Tomorrow will be soon enough
To run and jump and play
But now we're getting sleepy
Let's dream the night away

Will you go to sleep before I do?
Will you close your eyes real tight?
Will you go to sleep before I do?
And snuggle all through the night?

If you should go to sleep
A little while before I do
I hope that you will realize
My dear friend that I love you

Will you go to sleep before I do?
Will you close your eyes real tight?
Will you go to sleep before I do?
And snuggle all through the night?

Will you go to sleep before I do?
Will you go to sleep before I do?
And snuggle all through the night?

This Lovely Night

The room is filled with silence
It's quiet as can be
And as you hold me tight
I sense the love you share with me

Outside the clouds may fill the sky
Or stars may sparkle bright
The moon may shine upon the world
Or it may rain all night

But in the silence of our room
Each thing will be alright
As long as we're together here
All through this lovely night

This lovely night, this lovely night
This lovely, lovely night
This lovely night

Your heart is beating softly
I hardly dare to speak
And as you hold me tight
I feel your breath upon my cheek

The images of our daytime
So quickly fade away
The things that we have found to share
Have made a lovely day

A tremble rushes through me
As you hold me tight
There's nowhere I would rather be
All through this lovely night

This lovely night, this lovely night
This lovely, lovely night
This lovely night

HARD TO FIND CITY
MOSS FOREST
KING NOGBURTS
WIZARD OF WEE GEE
GRUNGES
TREMBLY FAULT
MUSHROOM FOREST
THE GREAT DESERT
Land of GRUNDO